I AM THE SOUTH AFRICAN SON

WRITTEN BY: JESSICA AMARO

AMARO GROUP
PUBLISHING

Mt Pleasant, SC
www.AmaroGroupServices.com
I AM THE SOUTH AFRICAN SON
©2023 Amaro Group Services LLC

Paperback ISBN: 978-1-961673-02-1

DEDICATION

"To Olivia, my brilliant shining 'star,' and Eddie, my extraordinary 'sun, you both light my path even on my darkest days."

AND

"To all the dreamers, believers, and young hearts with the courage to reach for the stars."

In a vibrant South African town,
Lived a boy with a sun-kissed crown.

Soaring high, with colors that never end,
A song so pure, echoing a dream within.

Colors unseen, and ideas so new,
A canvas of dreams in every shade of blue.

He painted the skies with his imagination,
"I'M AN AMAZING CREATION!"

A beautiful spirit dancing on solid ground,
Moving forward, dreams to be found.

Deep roots and with limbs that grew free,
A spirit maturing , dreams as vast as the sea.

Smiling his confidence unwavering and grand,

"I'M AS FREE AS LEAVES FLOATING
OVER OCEANS AND SAND!"

Each step he took, his kindness was steadfast,
Guided by love, and dreams bigger than the past.

Climbing mountains with purpose and a plan,

"I'M AS PERSISTENT AS THE STONES THAT SHAPED OUR LAND!"

Strong and gentle, a rare blend indeed,
Dreams and visions fueled his every need.

Near towering mountains, he'd often stroll with ease,
"I'M AS KIND AS NIGHT'S BREEZE
DANCING WITH THE TREES!"

In moments of rush, he remained so calm,
Dreams held close, wrapped securely in his palm.

Beneath the sky, watching the moon so bright,
"I AM AS EXTRAORDINARILY WONDROUS
AS THE STARLIT NIGHT!"

Guided by hopes and good seeds sown,
His dreams and hopes had truly grown.

With each passing year, his spirit took on a glow,

**"I'M AS RESILIENT AS THE SOIL,
LETTING LIFE FLOW!"**

In the heart of South Africa,
where stories are written in gold,
There stands a man that was once a boy,
his voice rich and bold.

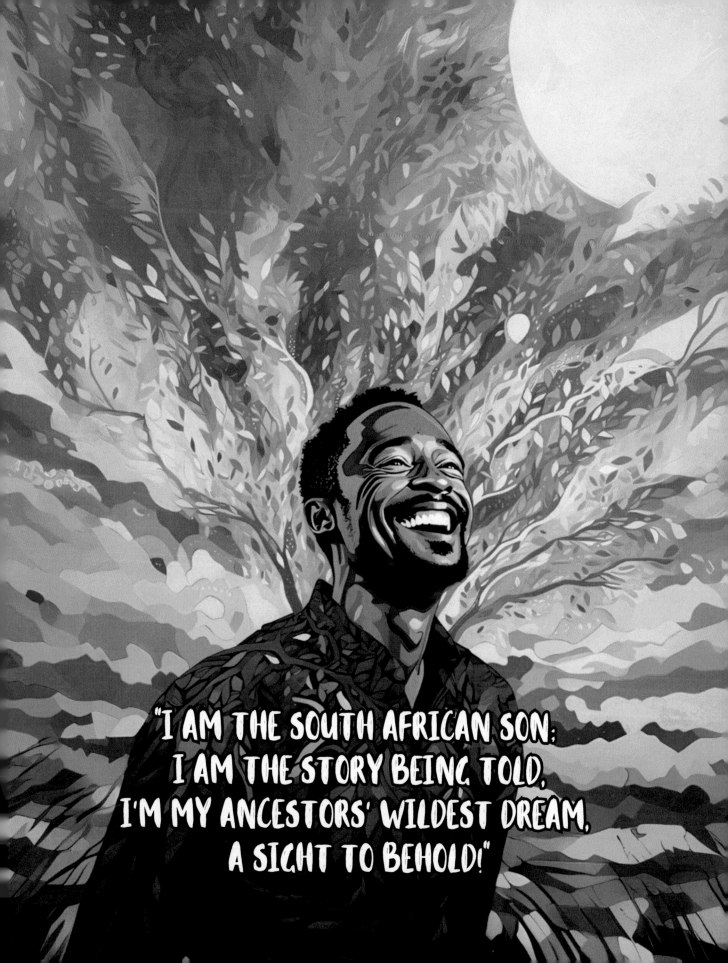

I AM THE SOUTH AFRICAN SON
RESOURCES

I AM THE SOUTH

In a vibrant South African town,
Lived a boy with a sun-kissed crown.
With each breath, his dreams took flight,
"I'm a tiny miracle, a shining light!"

Soaring high, with colors that never end,
A song so pure, echoing a dream within.
Each morning, he'd rise with the sun,
"I'm as free as a bird, my journey has just begun!"

Colors unseen, and ideas so new,
A canvas of dreams in every shade of blue.
He painted the skies with his imagination,
"I'm an amazing creation!"

A beautiful spirit dancing on solid ground,
Moving forward, dreams to be found.
Running, arms stretched wide and high,
"I'm unstoppable, like the wind and the sky!"

Deep roots and limbs that grew free,
A spirit maturing, dreams as vast as the sea.
Smiling, his confidence unwavering and grand,
"I'm as free as leaves floating over oceans and sand!"

AFRICAN SON

Each step he took, his kindness was steadfast,
Guided by love, and dreams bigger than the past.
Climbing mountains with purpose and a plan,
"I'm as persistent as stones that shaped our land!"

Strong and gentle, a rare blend indeed,
Dreams and visions fueled his every need.
Near towering mountains, he'd often stroll with ease,
"I'm as kind as night's breeze dancing with the trees!"

In moments of rush, he remained so calm,
Dreams held close, wrapped securely in his palm.
Beneath the sky, watching the moon so bright,
"I am as extraordinarily wondrous as the starlit night!"

Guided by hopes and good seeds sown,
His dreams and hopes had truly grown.
With each passing year, his spirit took on a glow,
"I'm as resilient as the soil, letting life flow!"

In the heart of South Africa, where stories are written in gold,
There stands a man that was once a boy, his voice rich and bold.
"I am the South African Son; I am the story being told,
I'm my ancestors' wildest dream, a sight to behold!"

-Jessica Amaro

I AM THE SOUTH AFRICAN SON
GLOSSARY

Let's bring clarity to the rich imagery and storytelling found in "I Am The South African Son." Within the verses on each page, you'll encounter a world of words, phrases, and concepts that hold deeper meanings and symbolism. As you read and explore, use this glossary to unlock these meanings Happy reading and discovery!

Ancestors: The people from the past, like grandparents and great-grandparents, who are a part of your family history.

Brilliance: When something is incredibly bright, like a shining star.

Canvas of Dreams: An idea that your mind creates, just like painting on a canvas.

Confidence: Feeling sure of yourself and your abilities.

Creation: Making something new or bringing an idea to life.

Dreams: The things you hope for or imagine happening.

Extraordinarily: Doing something in an amazing or very special way.

Imagination: When you think of things in your mind that are not real but can be very creative.

Nature's Beauty: The aesthetic qualities of the natural world, including elements like the sun, rainbow, and stars.

Persistence: When you keep trying, even when things are difficult.

Positive Self-Reflection: The practice of thinking positively about oneself and one's abilities.

Resilience: Being strong and able to bounce back from tough times.

Roots: The history and background of where you come from, like your family and culture.

Spirit: The part of you that makes you who you are and gives you energy.

Sun: In the poem, represents not only the sun in the sky that provides light and warmth but also serves as a symbol of hope, positivity, and the potential for growth.

Symbolism in Poetry: The use of symbols to represent ideas or qualities in poetry.

Unwavering: Refers to something that doesn't change or falter, remaining steady and strong.

Vast: Extremely big or wide.

Wildest Dream: Your biggest and most exciting dream.

Words and Emotions: How the words and emotions in the poem connect to the boy's journey and experiences.

DISCUSSION QUESTIONS

Welcome to the discussion questions for "I Am The South African Sun." These questions are designed to help you engage with the poem and explore its themes, symbols, and messages. The questions are divided into three age groups: Primary Readers , Secondary Readers, and Advanced Readers. Additionally, there is a section on for "All Readers," to encourage positive self-reflection and empowerment.

PRIMARY READERS

Dreaming Big: What are some of the dreams and aspirations you have, just like the young boy in the poem? Can you draw a picture of one of your dreams?

Nature's Beauty: What is your favorite part of nature mentioned in the poem, like the sun, the rainbow, or the stars? Why do you like it?

Exploring Emotions: How do you think the boy in the poem feels when he talks about being free and unstoppable? Can you use words to describe those feelings?

SECONDARY READERS

Figurative Language and Symbols: Discuss the figurative language and symbols used in the poem, such as the sun and the son. What do you think they represent, and how do they add depth to the story?

Persistence and Resilience: Explore the lines that talk about being persistent and resilient. Can you think of a time when you faced a challenge and had to be persistent? How did you feel afterward?

Words and Emotions: How do the words and emotions in the poem connect to the boy's journey and experiences? How does the author use language to convey these emotions?

ADVANCED READERS

Symbolism in Poetry: Analyze the use of symbolism in the poem, particularly with "sun" and "son." How do these symbols contribute to the poem's overall message?

Literary Techniques: Discuss the literary techniques used in the poem, such as metaphors, repetition, and imagery. How do these techniques enhance the poem's impact and meaning?

Interpreting Motivation: The poem is full of affirmations and motivation. Why do you think the author chose to include these affirmations in the poem? How do they contribute to the overall theme?

AFFIRMATIONS ALL READERS (AFFIRMATIONS)

Positive Self-Reflection: The poem is full of positive affirmations, such as "I'm unstoppable" and "I'm an amazing creation." Can you create your own affirmations that make you feel confident and inspired?

Encouraging Others: How can positive affirmations like those in the poem help you and others in your life to stay motivated and believe in your dreams?

Daily Affirmation Practice: Consider incorporating affirmations into your daily routine. Whether it's starting the day with a positive statement or using affirmations to overcome challenges, discuss how these daily practices can influence your mindset and actions. Share your favorite affirmations and how they impact your attitude and behavior throughout the day.

Note to Readers

"Thank you for embarking on this poetic journey through 'I AM THE SOUTH AFRICAN SON.' This poem celebrates the resilience of the human spirit, the power of dreams, and the connection to one's roots. May you find inspiration and strength in the story of a boy who became a man, a South African Son, and a living testament to the dreams of his ancestors. As you explore this poem, remember that you too are capable of remarkable things, and your journey is just beginning. Just as poems can transform into books, your dreams have the potential to become reality."

-Jessica Amaro

Made in the USA
Middletown, DE
16 October 2023